Ju
F
El 5 Ellentuck, Shan.
        Yankel the fool.

YANKEL THE FOOL

YANKEL THE FOOL

STORY & PICTURES BY SHAN ELLENTUCK

DOUBLEDAY & CO., INC. GARDEN CITY, NEW YORK

ISBN: 0-385-06533-7 Trade
     0-385-07524-3 Prebound
Library of Congress Catalog Card Number 71-175369
Copyright © 1973 by Merna Ellentuck
Printed in the United States of America
First Edition

CONTENTS

I   YANKEL THE FOOL   5

II   YANKEL THE TRAVELER   16

III   YANKEL THE BEGGAR   28

IV   THE NEXT CHAPTER   45

V   A BRIDE FOR YANKEL   49

VI   YANKEL THE THIEF   63

VII   YANKEL AND THE
WONDER-WORKING RABBI   75

VIII   MAZEL TOV!   85

The Recording Angel works like the very devil —
you should pardon the expression. He's up till all
hours of the night going over his books. Meanwhile
his deputies, the angels who work under him, fly
around the countryside keeping track of what's
going on — and then — just before dinner, they
report to the boss.

That's his worst hour. There he sits, in a crush
of yelling, shoving angels, each one in a hurry to
get to the table. The angel with the loudest voice

gets heard first — and he has a list as long as a rabbi's beard. He starts out: "Reb Malik gave a ruble and his old black pants to the beggar Avram." The Recording Angel smiles and pastes a gold star on the page next to Reb Malik's name. "Frodl pinched Yenta under the table." A black cross next to Frodl's name — the little witch! And so it goes.

By the time the angel from *our* district gets in a word, the soup's cold and all the best pieces of chicken are gone. Our angel is in a fury. He rattles off his list like an auctioneer! The Recording Angel can hardly keep up with him.

Of course, Yankel Schlimazel's name comes up right away. What has he done now? He stole a pair of gold earrings, a string of pearls, a bracelet, two rings and a few more things. There is an item-ized account. The boss sighs and dips his pen in the inkpot.

But hold on a minute — what's the hurry? Before he puts another black mark against Yankel's name in the Book of Heaven, let my friend the Recording Angel consider this: The man always tried hard to make an honest living. He's an orphan. His parents, may they rest in peace for eternity, left him nothing but debts. He has an old grand-mother to feed.

Isn't it a fact of life that it's easier for one to steal than for two to starve? I'm asking you! And is it Yankel's fault that he was born such a FOOL?

In the days before he came to this earth, when he was still being patted into shape, it's true he was given all the usual things — two arms, two legs, a belly, a heart, a head. Maybe his head was too small, or maybe it was carelessness, but when his brain was stuffed in, something got left out. Horse sense! He's got no more horse sense than a sunflower! But I ask you — was this *his* fault? Believe me, he never blamed the Recording Angel for his troubles, so why should the dear angel blame him?

I'll tell you more about Yankel Schlimazel. His nose was put in the middle of his face, his hair is as straight and black as a driving rain, and his name — Schlimazel — means nothing more or less than "bad luck." With a name like that who could prosper in this world? "Schlimazel" followed Yankel like a big black billy goat — always ready to butt him in the behind.

Already you feel sorry for the poor man. You're like me — always ready to stick up for the underdog. I tell you — I swear to you — at heart this Yankel was always an honest man. There's a story behind it, and if you'll let me get on with the story you can decide for yourself. I just hope the angel from our district is listening in. If he'd think more about justice in heaven and less about supper . . . !

I. YANKEL THE FOOL

So. When he was still a boy, and already the man
of his household, Yankel became apprentice to the
village baker. Every morning before daybreak he
rose and ran through the black and muddy streets,
with the frost nipping at his heels, to start the
ovens and sweep the floor.

That was the year of the drought, and the next
year was the second year of the drought, and the
third year was the year of the floods. In three
years there wasn't enough grain harvested to feed

5

a small family of mice. No grain means no flour. No flour means no bread. No bread means no work for the baker.

"Listen, Yankele," said the wretched baker, "Why don't you become a tailor? Even a starving man has to cover his nakedness."

So Yankel Schlimazel rose before daylight and scuttled through the village, waking up the cocks that crowed dawn, and until nightfall he picked up pins and rolled heavy bolts of woolen cloth and swept the tailor's shop. He worked like a slave. Was it his fault that the bad years had left everyone poor? A poor man patches his pants. He doesn't buy new ones.

"What can I say?" sighed the tailor. "Go find a new master. Peace be with you, and if you get rich, remember me kindly, eh?"

But in those days who needed another mouth to feed? There was no work anywhere, for anyone. Yankel went to his grandmother with empty hands and a sad face.

"If you can't work for anyone else — work for yourself," the old woman told him. And she gave him the little bit of money she had saved for her funeral, to set him up in business. "Buy fish at the river for two kopeks apiece," she advised him, "and sell them in the market place for three. What you don't sell we can eat!"

With the coins in the toe of his boot, Yankel went down to the river's edge, where the fishermen were drawing in their nets. There was one man there as fat as a wagon horse. "In a lean year a fat man is a good sign!" Yankel said, and to this man he went to do business.

"Excuse me, uncle," he said politely, just to start the conversation. "Are you in the fish business?"

This fisherman was a big joker. "No, my boy," he said, "I'm trying to catch bears."

Yankel's mouth dropped open. "Bears?" he cried. "What kind of bears?"

"Black bears, brown bears," said the man, "and maybe, if I have a bit of luck — maybe polar bears."

"I never heard of such a thing! Wait till I tell my grandmother. She'll never believe it!"

"Numskull!" laughed the man. "Idiot! Fool! Rattlebrain! Do you believe everything that comes out of anybody's mouth? Can't you see for yourself that I'm a fisherman?"

Yankel sat down on a rock and began to weep out loud. "It's true!" he sobbed, "I believe everything. I'm the biggest dolt in the world."

The fat fisherman looked slyly at Yankel. "I

know a sure way to cure a fool," he said. "Why should you suffer? Do what I tell you and I promise, my boy, you'll be smarter in five minutes."

"Anything, uncle!" Yankel agreed joyfully. "Anything you say!"

"You know," said the man, "that fish is considered brain food. And what part of the fish is the best for this business? Why the head, of course! As a special favor I will sell you a fish head for only three kopeks." And with that he pulled a plump herring from his net and whacked off its head with one blow of his knife. "Here you are. Pay and eat — and a good appetite to you!"

You shouldn't think about what happened next. A raw fish head is no pleasure — not even for a hungry boy — but Yankel forced it down in two gulps.

"Do you feel anything?" asked the fisherman.

"Not in my head," said Yankel.

"Then lie down on the grass for a while. Your brain will begin to work by itself," the man said, and he went back to pulling on the net.

Yankel lay on the ground and stared up at the sky. Sure enough, his brain started working, and this is what was on his mind. One whole fish costs two kopeks. The fish head cost him three kopeks. For two kopeks he could have had a fish for the soup pot, a fish head for the brain, and a kopek left over. He jumped up and let out a yell. "You thief," he shouted. "You cheat! You fooled me!"

"You see," laughed the fisherman, "it works like a charm! Tell the truth — aren't you smarter already?"

Well, in a manner of speaking, it was true. So Yankel, with his new-found wisdom, and the rest of the money in his boot, bought a basket of fish from the fat joker and carried it off to the market, where he sat himself down in comfort and waited for business.

The day was hot and soon the fish began to give off a smell that was more than the boy could bear. "How can the fish-sellers live with such a stench?" he asked himself. "They must stuff their noses with rags! If I don't get rid of this basket I'll faint dead away for sure!" So he looked around the market place until he found an old woman who was selling a goose and some goslings. "Aunty," he shouted, "how would you like some fish? I'll sell them nice and cheap."

"I haven't a kopek," croaked the old woman. "Come back when I've sold my goslings, eh?"

"No," said Yankel. "That long I can't wait. But

why don't you trade me the goslings for the fish right now?"

"The goslings are worth more than the fish, my boy."

They bargained back and forth and the upshot of the talk was this: Yankel got the goslings and the old woman got the fish and a promise of four more fish when the day was done.

The boy carried off his baby geese with great pleasure, but he soon found them a terrible burden. Not for a minute could he turn his back without having one of the little creatures running away. In the hot sun he was chasing them all over the market.

Along came a man with a basket of eggs. He stopped to watch Yankel struggling with the goslings, and he laughed so hard that the eggs rattled like cannon balls. "Don't make fun of me, uncle!" the boy called out. "Trade me your eggs for my pretty little geese before my poor legs fall off from all this running!"

"I'll do that," said the man, "and gladly! But you can see my basket is full and there aren't as many goslings as eggs!"

Well they finally came to an agreement. Yankel got the eggs and gave the man — not only his gos-

lings — but the promise of one more gosling when the day was at an end.

But before he had a chance to make a single kopek, Yankel saw a pretty girl struggling up the hill with a great sack of potatoes. "Let me help you!" he cried, and with the basket of eggs joggling on his arm he ran down to meet her.

"If you could help me get rid of these potatoes it would be a blessing," said the girl. "I'm ready to faint from the heat." And she smiled so sweetly at Yankel that it addled his brain. "Take my eggs to sell," he offered, "and I'll sell the potatoes. What do you say?"

"My father would beat me if I made such a bargain," the pretty girl said. "How can I trade a big sack for a little basket?"

But it was soon arranged. "The minute I've made a bit of money I'll get another dozen eggs for you," said Yankel, and he threw the sack across his back. It weighed a ton.

"Buy a pickle!" cried the pickle man. "Yankel, Yankel — pickles give you strength. Yankel, Yankel — buy my juicy pickles!"

Oh, those pickles looked like the fruit of heaven to the boy, and he didn't have a single copper coin to call him father. "Will you give me a pickle if I give you a potato?" he begged. "Or better yet — will you give me all the pickles for all the potatoes?"

As before, the trade was made after a little bargaining back and forth. "So you'll remember you owe me five more potatoes, eh, Yankel?" said the man. "Big ones with no soft spots, do you hear? And make sure I get them before the sun goes down!"

Yankel made free with the crock of pickles. Two he sold and one he ate, three he sold and two he ate, and so on until his belly ached, the crock was empty and his pocket was full. Then he turned the crock top side down, and, leaning his back against it, slept in peace until late afternoon.

The sun was across the river when he awoke, and the market place was emptying. Poor Yankel sat up in a fright. "The day is gone — and I haven't kept any of my bargains!" He ran off to get some fish for the woman who had traded him the goslings, but there were none to be found. "Aunty," he cried to her, "I promised to give you four more fish but there isn't even a fin left in the market place. What can I do?"

"A bargain is a bargain!" cried the old woman. "Give me twelve kopeks and I'll find my own!"

"Twelve!" shouted Yankel. "I'll give you eight!"

So they settled on ten and wished each other a good night. Then Yankel set off in search of a gosling for the egg man. He could find only one and the fellow selling it asked a pretty price — but there was nothing the boy could do. "All right," he said at last, "but you're nothing better than a thief!" And he ran off before he was clobbered.

It was no easier to buy the eggs — and the potatoes were harder yet to find. It cost Yankel a little fortune to pay off the load of his debts and he went home at sunset with less in his pocket than he had at sunrise. And what did he have to show for a hard day's work? An empty pickle crock and a long sad story to tell his grandmother!

"Yankele, Yankele," the good old woman said, sighing. "A businessman you'll never be!" And she went next door to a neighbor's house to borrow a potato for supper!

II. YANKEL THE TRAVELER

Things got so bad at Yankel's house that it was hard to believe they could get worse. The boy and his grandmother lived from hand to mouth. From one holiday to the next they didn't see a piece of meat on the table. It was potatoes for breakfast and potatoes for supper — and in between? — in between it was cold air! Now and then Yankel earned a few kopeks doing odd jobs, and time and again some kind neighbor took from her own pot to feed them.

Finally this hard life was too much for the old grandmother. First she shriveled up like a dried apple, and then she took to her bed, groaning and moaning, with pains in her head and aches in her legs.

Straightaway Yankel ran to the doctor and begged him to look at the old woman. "I have nothing to give you for your trouble," he cried, "but I have strong arms. I'll work for you until the fee is paid!"

The doctor took one look at Yankel's arms — like kindling wood they were — and he sighed. Listen, he had more poor patients than a horse has horseflies. But he was a good man and he went along to look at the old lady. He gave her, from his own pocket, some money for medicine. He sent her, from his own table, chicken soup and white bread to build up her strength.

"Don't worry, little mother," he promised, "you'll recover. But you'll have to take it easy! You're not growing any younger you know!"

"So?" whispered the old grandmother, "who asks to grow younger? God willing, I only hope to grow a little older!"

When the Angel of Death, who was standing by the side of her bed, heard the old woman joking with the doctor, he shouldered his knapsack

full of worn-out souls and went looking for a more sorrowful household.

Sure enough the grandmother got better, and soon she was up and about, sweeping the floor and sitting in the sun with her mending on her lap. "Now," she said to Yankel, "go to the doctor and pay our debt!"

This doctor was well-to-do and he had a whole houseful of servants to work for him. He could think of nothing for Yankel to do. Still Yankel pestered him with offers of help until the good man thought he would go out of his mind. All day long the boy sat on the doorstep, like a big rag doll, waiting for a chance to speak to the doctor. The patients had to step over him to get inside. The doctor's wife added her voice to Yankel's. "Find something for that boy to do," she nagged, "or he'll turn to stone on the stairs!"

At last a passing angel blew an idea into the doctor's ear. "Listen," said the man, "I have a brother living in the next town. If you'll go to his house and deliver a birthday gift to him, I'll be repaid in full!"

"Agreed!" cried Yankel cheerfully, and he took from the good man a beautiful silver goblet wrapped in a woolen shirt. For a kindness, bless his name, the doctor also gave Yankel a hunk of bread and a piece of cheese to eat on the way.

The boy hurried home to kiss his grandmother good-by. His heart was singing with joy, for you must know that although the town was only a day's walk from his home, Yankel had never been there in his life. What stories he had heard about that place! It was said to be ten times the size of their little village, with paved streets and enormous buildings and all sorts of marvels such as are promised for the cities of heaven!

Yankel was all set to start out that very day, but his grandmother would have none of such nonsense. First he was sent to the bathhouse while his clothing was carted off to the river, beaten clean on the stones and hung on a tree branch to dry. His boots needed blacking — never mind the holes in the bottom — and the grandmother dug around in her dower chest to find a piece of cloth to wrap around the fine woolen shirt that was wrapped around the silver goblet so nothing should get dirty or torn.

It was morning before everything was ready to the grandmother's satisfaction. On Yankel's back the package was tied and lunch was in his pocket. For fear of dirtying his polished boots on the dusty road, the boy carried them in his hand. He waved to everyone he passed. "I'm going to town!" he cried, "I'm off to town!"

Well, a day's walk takes up a day, no matter how you look at it. All morning Yankel marched along, singing to himself and going over in his mind everything he had ever heard about the town. He added a little here and a little there until, by noontime, he had in his mind's eye such wonders as never were — no, not even in the days of King Solomon! He was going to see streets paved with gold and buildings that hid their chimney pots in the clouds! All the horses — he imagined — were snow white, and the garbage carts were gilded and painted with flowers!

Such dreaming was enough to put anyone to sleep and by the time the sun was above his head, Yankel could hardly sing for all his yawning. "So I'll have my bread and cheese," he said to himself, "and a little nap under a tree. Then I'll start out fresh and be at the house of the doctor's brother before dark."

Now, Yankel was a bit of a fool — a great deal of a fool — but not *all* of a fool, and before he lay down in the grass to sleep he put his boots carefully by the side of the road with their toes pointed straight toward the town. "That way," he explained to himself, "I'll be sure to set out in the right direction when I wake up."

Very pleased with his wisdom, Yankel was snoring before the last bite of bread and cheese was down his gullet.

The tall grass hid Yankel from sight completely. Along came a peasant in a cart on his way to the market. He saw nothing and nobody — but a pair of shiny boots by the side of the road — and at once he stopped his horse and jumped down to get this great prize.

The minute he picked them up, however, the peasant let out an angry cry. "These aren't boots — they're fish nets! The ants underneath can see the sky! If I put them on my feet I could draw them up to my thighs!" And, in disgust, he dropped the boots and wasted no more time getting on with his journey. Unfortunately, the toes of the boots now pointed straight toward the village which Yankel had just left.

And what happened then? Yankel woke, stretched and made ready to take to the road again. "Fish heads make a man wise indeed!" he said proudly, and he set off in the direction his boots pointed out.

"Isn't that interesting," said Yankel to himself.

"I passed a rock just like that one this morning. And I saw a tree that was brother to that tree." A little farther along, a dog lay dozing by the side of the road. "Hello!" cried Yankel. "You must be worn out! I passed you hours ago and here you are ahead of me already!"

Before long the boy could see houses in the distance. He clapped his hands with delight, but as he got closer and closer his heart grew troubled. Was this the great town? There were nothing but huts, such as he knew from his own village! There — there was one just like the tailor's, and there was a stable that was not one bit different from the one he had passed at daybreak! He peered into a stall and his mouth dropped open. Was there a snow-white mare inside, fit for a king to ride? Don't believe it — the horse was brown, the horse was dirty, and the back of this nag dipped like a soupspoon between his stringy tail and his tangled mane.

Everywhere Yankel looked there was a fresh disappointment. "What liars those traveling men are!" he said with a sigh. "How can they call this poor miserable little mud hole a place of many wonders? Why this town and my village are two calves from the same cow!"

Still, Yankel could not stand around forever

sighing and crying. He had an important package to deliver and he set his mind to finding the right house.

"Since this place is so much like my own village, it stands to reason that the doctor and his brother would live in houses very much alike," Yankel decided. He went up one dusty street and down another. Everywhere he walked people called greetings to him. Every face was familiar — and after much thought Yankel said to himself, "The townspeople are a friendly bunch. Why they speak to me as if they've known me all my life. People are not so different in this world after all!"

Within a few minutes Yankel found the house for which he was searching. "The very one!" he cried. "Exactly the same as the doctor's — down to the flowers at the doorstep."

Unstrapping the package from his back, the boy walked up to the front door and knocked as boldly as a soldier. Who should open the door but a man with a napkin around his neck and a chicken wing in his hand!

"Imagine!" muttered Yankel. "You would think that the doctor could tell me this brother was his twin! There isn't a hair in his beard that's the least bit different!

Out loud he said politely, "Peace be with you.

25

I am Yankel Schlimazel and I bring you a birthday gift from your brother, the doctor in my village. May you have a thousand birthdays and all in the best of health!"

Just think of the poor boy's surprise when the man in the doorway began to howl with laughter. He roared, he choked, he slapped his thighs — and the chicken wing flew out of his hand and into the street where a cat made his supper out of it before you could say "God bless you!"

Well, that night Yankel also dined at the doctor's table and at least part of the mystery was solved. "Though I don't understand what went wrong," said Yankel sadly, "and I suppose I never will!"

Put it down to the doctor's kind heart that he sent Yankel off the next day with a peasant who was going to the town and Yankel rode in a cart there and back and delivered the gift and saw what little was to be seen. The good doctor never said a word to anybody, though he got the name for being a little bit crazy from then on. Why? Because every time he saw Yankel Schlimazel he had a fit — laughing, choking and slapping his thighs — until whatever was in his hand flew out as if it had chicken wings and landed in the dirt of the street!

III. YANKEL THE BEGGAR

Things changed slowly in the village. The baker was kicked by a horse and limped ever afterward. The tailor's eldest son ran off to America. Rivke, the rabbi's beautiful daughter, became engaged to the doctor's nephew, but there was some disagreement between the families and the engagement was called off. What more? Some died, and some were born. I tell you the truth; things changed slowly in the village.

Now, Yankel was not a child any more. To begin with, he was growing like a tree by the side of the water. His arms and legs were as long and skinny as willow branches, and he could touch the eaves of the roof without standing on a stool. In short — he was tall; he was a man!

So you tell me — what is the biggest difference between a boy and a man? It's simple — a man eats more than a boy! Perhaps for some people the years were fatter, but for Yankel and his grandmother each day was a skinnier chicken than the day before. Finally the old woman spoke seriously to her grandson.

"It's no shame to be poor."

"That's true," said Yankel, "but it's no great honor, either."

"It's a blessing on a man's head to help the needy," the grandmother continued. "Every kopek a rich man puts in the hands of a poor man goes down in the Book of Heaven as a star next to his name."

"That's true also," Yankel agreed. "But why are we discussing philosophy today?"

The old grandmother sighed. "I think the time has come when you should help the rich to collect their blessings. What could it hurt to ask for a little here and a little there?"

"What?" cried Yankel. "You want me to become

a beggar — a schnorrer? Never! I'll die first!"

"And who's going to pay for your coffin?" wept the grandmother. "And who's going to pay for mine?"

So Yankel Schlimazel became a schnorrer — or rather he became an apprentice to a schnorrer, for begging is a trade that has to be learned like any other.

Labl the Lame took him on as an assistant. It was Yankel's job to carry the sack, and, when they came to a stream, Labl would hop on Yankel's back and be carried across without wetting his toes.

This Labl was a clever man, a proud man, an expert at his work. He had a tongue like a violin — it could play whatever tune he thought you might dance to! Labl spoke gently and sweetly, and the women, with their soft hearts, wept to hear of his misfortunes and heaped food in his sack and money in his hands. With a meek man he roared like a crazy bull — and came away so much the richer!

At the first house they visited together, the cripple told Yankel to hide behind a tree. "Watch what I do and hear what I say. You are learning your trade from a master!" Then, with his big hands he beat on the door as if the house were on fire.

Right away a man came running to see who was there, and without a word Labl held out his cap for a little charitable donation. It so happens that the man had been sleeping, and he was in no mood for charity. "Get out of here!" he shouted. "All day long I'm bothered by you schnorrers! Why don't you work for a living? You have a head on your shoulders!"

You think Labl the Lame was frightened off by such a greeting? "So?" he said with a mocking smile. "You give your money only to headless men? And the fathers of orphans? And flying cows? What a peasant you are!" He laughed in scorn.

"Forgive me, forgive me," the man said. "I didn't mean to offend you. Here's a kopek, my good man, and peace be with you."

"I have an apprentice!" said Labl, pointing to Yankel, who was hidden in the leaves. Without a word the man dug in his pocket for another kopek.

"And with you, peace!" Labl sang out in a voice like a sugar cake with raisins.

Then the two, the beggar and his boy, went off to the house of a well-to-do miller. A servant girl let them in. "My master is busy," she said, "and he has no time for you today. Go on, try the next house!"

Well! You might have thought the girl had poured boiling water on Labl's head. He screamed! He fell to the floor! He beat his crutch on the furniture and raised such a noise that the geese outside the door began to honk in terror. Not one word did he say — but does a hungry lion have to talk?

The miller was out of his room in a minute. "Stop that!" he cried. "I'm trying to do business with an important official! What is he going to think? Here — here's a whole ruble. Now clear out at once!"

"A blessing on your head, uncle," said Labl sweetly, as Yankel helped him to his feet and dusted off his rags. "May your business prosper and your wife fill the house with pretty children." And he bowed like a gentleman.

The angry miller wanted the last word. "Let me give you a piece of advice. If you hadn't made such a racket I would have given you two rubles tomorrow!" Labl, who was already out the door and halfway down the path, laughed out loud. "Listen, uncle," he called over his shoulder. "Do you think *I* can afford to give credit? I don't tell you how to run your mill — don't you give me advice on how to be a beggar!" And he put the ruble in his pocket and picked a blossom from the miller's garden for his buttonhole!

Don't think for a minute that every kopek was so hard to come by. There are plenty of God's angels walking around this earth in shoe leather! Labl made himself a living, and though he paid Yankel little enough, a little is enough when you're used to nothing! The old grandmother was able to save a coin here and there. "What did I tell you?" she said to Yankel. "You can get rich being poor!"

At last the day came when Labl the Lame decided that Yankel's apprenticeship was over. "It's time you went into business for yourself," he said. "Tomorrow we visit Reb Itzak the Miser. If you can wheedle a loaf of bread — a slice of bread — a crust of bread — even a crumb — out of the old man you'll be worthy of the name of schnorrer!"

Let me tell you a thing or two about this miser. About the time Yankel was choking on a fish head on the riverbank, Reb Itzak came back from America to live in the village where he had been born. In America, the old women said, he and his brother had made a fortune selling secondhand clothes. The old women also said that he cheated his brother out of every penny the poor man owned — but who listens to such gossip?

Now why would a man, such a rich man, want to live in a muddy village in the middle of no-place?

Don't ask me. Rich men are often very peculiar. It is enough to say that he came back and had a house built for himself as fine as a palace. He had servants, a horse and carriage, a coat trimmed with fur, leather boots as soft as silk, chicken at every meal, wine with every chicken and — listen to this — his wife wore pearls to go to market!

But what pleasure did it give the man? If he had to spend a kopek he first kissed it good-by. When his house was finished and the workmen came for their pay, Reb Itzak's scraggly beard was green from kissing copper coins!

A rich man is like honey to the bears, and in this case the bears were the beggars who knocked on his door day and night, crying for charity. His servants turned them away with kicks and curses. You would think these people might get discouraged and stop coming? Please — use your head! First of all there weren't so many millionaires that they could pick and choose. Second — it was a challenge — a matter of professional pride for a schnorrer to snatch a kopek from such a tight fist. And last of all — well there was no last of all — the first two reasons were enough!

I'll tell you more about this miser. Reb Itzak bought the best horse in the countryside. He paid a fortune for it, but once it was his, it hurt his heart to see that animal eat. The horse ate like a horse, what can I tell you? Finally the old man had a marvelous idea! Every day he gave the horse less feed. "He'll learn to do with almost nothing," the man told himself. "And if he's smart, in good time he'll learn to do without!"

The nag got skinnier and skinnier. One day he lay down and died. Reb Itzak was in a rage. "That's the gratitude you can expect from a stupid animal!" he howled. "Here I've taught him to live on air and he pays me back by dying!"

So now you know what Yankel was up against?

Like a couple of generals going into battle, Labl and his apprentice sat down and planned their campaign. That Labl — you should only have such a brain — he hatched a scheme that was worthy of the devil himself. Not that an angel couldn't have thought it up, of course — it's just that the devil has more reason to set his mind to scheming.

From the pickle-man's second son, who had just gotten married, Yankel borrowed a fine, clean, new coat. He blacked his boots and washed his hair. "Look at him!" cried the old grandmother. "He could be the Prince of Schnorrers!"

At dinnertime the next day, the master and the apprentice went to the rich man's house. As he had been taught to do, Yankel knocked boldly on the door while Labl, like a servant, stood behind him carrying the sack. A fat woman stuck her head out the window and shouted, "Go away! The master has nothing here for you!"

"What do you take me for?" Yankel shouted back. "Do I look like a schnorrer? Tell your master that I've come on business."

Reb Itzak's face appeared in the window. He looked Yankel up and down as if he were a cow in the market place. "All right, let him in," he said finally. "Business is business, and I can talk to him while I'm eating."

Yankel was very polite. He put on the manners of a nobleman. He wiped his feet before he entered the house and bowed low to the master. "Peace be with you, uncle," said Yankel, taking a chair at the table as though he were in his own house. "Don't let me interrupt your dinner. I see you're having gefilte fish? My favorite dish!"

With a bone-handled silver knife, the miser spread chicken fat on a slice of bread and stuffed the whole thing into his mouth. Crumbs sprinkled his chin and the fat greased his puffy red lips. As rich as he was, he was a dirty old man. "So you like gefilte fish?" he said slyly. "How do you feel about COLD gefilte fish?"

"It's the only way to eat it!" Yankel cried. "With

a little slice of carrot, a little dab of horseradish. You couldn't ask for anything better on this earth than a plate of nice cold gefilte fish!"

"Too bad!" sniggered the miser. "*This* fish is steaming — right out of the pot, so I won't offer you any."

What could Yankel say? His mouth was watering, but it was clear he would have to sing for his supper. Anyway, there was work to be done. "Uncle," he said, "you aren't looking so bad after all!"

"And what does *that* mean?" mumbled the old man, picking his teeth with a fish bone.

"It means what it says, uncle. After all the things I've heard I didn't hope to find you looking so well. A little pale maybe . . ." said Yankel, laying his tanned hand alongside the miser's chubby white fingers. "But for a man your age — in your condition. . . ."

"What are you talking about?" cried the miser. "I'm in the best of health!"

Yankel nodded his head wisely. "Of course you are! Of course you are! Your stomach is better, isn't it? And your appetite? How's your appetite? Are you sleeping well? As long as you feel fine, what difference does it make what the doctor says!"

The old man turned white. Without thinking,

he spread chicken fat on another piece of bread, but it lay there on the table untouched. "What does the doctor say?" he whispered. "The stomach pains — what does the doctor say about those?"

"Don't disturb yourself, uncle," said Yankel with a cheerful laugh. "You know those medical men, they're always talking about the worst! Well, what do you say we get down to business, eh?"

"Wait a minute!" cried Reb Itzak. He laid a trembling hand on the young man's arm. "What does the doctor say? I'm sick? I'm dying?"

Yankel leaned over, picked up the bread and bit off a corner. The finest white bread, the best chicken fat! Oh, how those millionaires eat! "Please," he said. "Don't ask me. First of all, I haven't spoken to your doctor personally. All I know is what I hear in the street."

The old miser let out a terrible groan and fell back in the chair with his hand over his heart. "It's all over! They're already putting nails in my coffin!"

There was a bowl of chicken and vegetables on the table. Yankel spooned some onto a couple of plates and motioned Labl to sit down. The two of them dug into the food greedily, but Reb Itzak neither saw nor said.

"Calm yourself!" mumbled Yankel between

bites. "A man like you has nothing to fear. Haven't you already paved your way to heaven with your wealth? By this time the angels have marked you down so often in the Book that they'll greet you by your first name. What's to worry? Your family is prepared. I myself heard from the tailor's daughter that your wife bought four yards of the finest black silk only last week. She won't shame you! And your son will be home next week, no?"

"He said he was coming home for the holidays — not for my funeral!" moaned the old man.

"Who said anything about a funeral? Why do you let your mind dwell on such things? Rejoice, Reb Itzak, you're a fortunate man. You'll have your family around you, very nicely dressed, and a seat dusted off in heaven!"

Let me tell you that all during this speech Labl and Yankel were making themselves free with the feast. Between the talking and the eating, Yankel was doing a fine job, and his master beamed at him proudly. "You're doing first-class work!" he whispered in the boy's ear. "I couldn't do better myself! Now quick — pluck the goose before he runs away!"

Yankel wiped his mouth carefully on a white linen napkin and leaned over close to the miser.

"What's bothering you, Reb Itzak? Have you done something so terrible that you're afraid? Nobody believes those stories about you — and besides, even if you've done a few things you'd like to forget, you must have enough good deeds to wipe up the stains. Think of all your charity! That counts for a lot!"

In a tiny voice, like the voice of a goldfish, Reb Itzak moaned, "What charity? Oh, my sins! They're pressing on my throat! They're squeezing the breath out of me!"

"Listen, uncle, it isn't too late. Do you want me to help you? I can't bear to see you suffer. Give me a few gold rubles, and I'll see to it that they get into the hands of the poor."

"Gold rubles?" cried the miser, turning green in his misery. "I can't throw money away!"

"That's true. You shouldn't be wasteful. Save it for your son, uncle. Don't worry about the next life."

The old man began to beat his hands on the table. "Leave my money to that no-good? He'll gamble it away!"

"All right, it's nothing to get excited about. How about your wife?"

"She'll spend it on jewels — on dresses — on

43

fancy furniture! Oh no — I'd rather give it to the poor! At least that way there's something in it for me! GIVE ME MY MONEYBAGS!"

So that's how it happened, just as I related it to you. Yankel went out from the miser's house with a handful of gold, and the miser took to his bed, prepared to die — though he's still living for all I know! It served him right — the scare he got. Maybe he's been a little freer with his money since that day, but if he is or if he isn't, it's no part of this story!

And what did Yankel do with the money? Half of it he gave to Labl, which was only fair, and half of what was left he gave to his old grandmother, who cried for joy, and half of what was left of that he spent on a fine, clean, new coat and boots with soles on them. And the rest? Well there was gefilte fish — cold and hot — every day for a week on Yankel's table, and, listening to his own advice he gave a few kopeks to the needy. Why shouldn't a poor fool go to heaven too?

IV. THE NEXT CHAPTER

As long as he kept his ears closed and his pockets buttoned, Yankel did well enough at his trade. It's true that he was a good schnorrer, but it was also true that money ran through his hands faster than he could pour it in. For one thing a whole troupe of beggars followed him around from house to house. As soon as he collected two kopeks, they talked him out of one or both. The stories they told him — and he — poor Yankel — he believed them! They even took bets, those lazy no-goods, on who could get the most out of Yankel! I'll give you an example.

One day Schmul One-Eye, weeping and wringing his hands, ran up to Yankel in the street. "Lend me a kopek, brother — just one kopek. My little daughter is sick, and I have to buy medicine. I'll pay you back, I swear, next week!"

Yankel had no use for Schmul One-Eye, but who was he to say no to a fellow human in great need? Frankly he never expected to see the kopek again.

So imagine his surprise and pleasure when the beggar came to him exactly one week later and pressed into his hand not one but two coins, and one of them bright, shiny, brand new. "Mazel tov," cried Schmul, "Congratulations! While I was on my way home my daughter got better, and I didn't have to spend the money for medicine after all. So I kept the coin in my coat pocket, and wonder of wonders — while it was in my pocket your lovely kopek had a baby! And here they are — mother and child!"

"What kind of story is this?" said Yankel. "Who ever heard of a copper coin having a baby?"

Schmul got very angry. "You don't believe me? You don't trust me? What have I ever done to you? I'm trying hard to be an honest man, and poor as

I am, and with all the troubles I carry on my shoulders it's no easy thing I can promise you, and you — you don't believe me! Am I supposed to keep the baby? If the mother is yours, the baby is yours!" And with that he stalked away.

The whole business bothered Yankel very much. For weeks, whenever he wasn't thinking about something else, he was thinking about the kopek who had a baby. Wonder of wonders, indeed!

So a month later Schmul One-Eye ran up to Yankel in the street and asked for the loan of a ruble. A whole gold ruble! "Listen," said Yankel to himself. "Who am I to say no? And who knows what will happen to my money in Schmul's pocket? Maybe I'll be grandfather to a new little ruble — or maybe twins? Wouldn't that be nice?"

But a week passed and two weeks. There wasn't a sign of Schmul. A month went by before the one-eyed man knocked on Yankel's door. He had on a very long face, and his good eye looked red, as though it had been weeping. "I have something terrible to tell you, brother," he said. "While I had your ruble at my house, it got sick. I nursed it like a baby, like one of my own little ones. But last night it took a turn for the worse, and this morning, just after breakfast the poor ruble — ah, the little darling — it died!"

"What?" yelled Yankel. "Who ever heard of a ruble dying?"

Schmul sighed again. "Why not?" he said. "If a kopek can have babies — why can't a ruble die?" And he went on his way, laughing so hard into his coat collar that he almost choked on the collar button!

V. A BRIDE FOR YANKEL

With tricks and stories like that, his fellow schnorrers kept Yankel in rags. Anyway, begging is no
business for a strong, healthy young man. At this
time the baker — and this is Avram the Baker who
was the boy's first master, the same baker who was
kicked by a horse and limped from then on — this
Avram was again looking for someone to help him
around the ovens.

"I can't pay you much," he said, "but I'm not a
young man — I'm a widower, and my wife and I

49

were never blessed with children. When I'm gone the business will be yours, and while I'm alive I'll treat you like a son."

So every Friday the old grandmother hobbled to the bakery and got two loaves of bread and all of Yankel's pay. "If it's not in your pocket, it can't fall out the bottom," she told him. The old woman was a good manager. Every week she put a few kopeks in a jar in a hole in the floor. "For when you get married," she explained.

Married? Who thought of getting married? Well, why not? Yankel was old enough. It's true he didn't have a beard yet. Ah, his father — his father had a beard, even as a young man, as thick as a wolf's tail, and it covered his chest so you never knew if he was wearing a shirt or not. Why shouldn't Yankel have such a beard? Didn't he in every other way take after his father, may he rest in peace? Didn't he have ears like his father's? A nose like his father's? Debts like his father's?

Then again, his mother, may she also rest in peace, God bless her, she was a good woman — his mother never had much in the way of hair on her face. It's entirely possible that Yankel took after his mother in this respect.

But we were talking about weddings, weren't we? I can assure you there were plenty of marriageable girls in the village. There was Rivke, the rabbi's beautiful daughter, and Roisl, the shoemaker's eldest. And Malka, Shifra, Tsipe and Yetta. All beautiful girls — and if they weren't beautiful they had kind hearts — and if they were mean, well they came from respectable families.

One morning, as they pounded the dough and shaped the loaves, Yankel talked it all over with Avram the Baker. "How should I go about it? What shall I say? You know me, I believe anything! Before I know it I'll be married off to a cat with ten kittens!"

"Don't worry," said Avram. "I'll be like a father to you, just as I promised. We'll go to see the matchmaker together. Just let me do all the talking, eh?"

So on the day arranged, Yankel put on his best clothes, as if he were calling on Reb Itzak the Miser, and the two of them set out to see the matchmaker. Velvel the Matchmaker lived in a little hut on the edge of town, but believe me, his eyes and ears were in the middle of everything. He knew to a handkerchief how much linen was in every girl's dower chest. Of course, like all matchmakers he had a great talent for making the best of everything, for saying the kindest thing in the kindest way, and for being blind to what he didn't want to see! To Velvel, all girls were beauties and all women were girls!

The three men sat around the table and drank the wine that Avram brought and ate the honey cake Yankel's grandmother had made for the occasion. Reb Velvel combed his stringy gray beard with his fingers and squinted his eyes. "There's the tailor's youngest girl. Can she cook! You should taste her potato pancakes — and her noodle pudding! She bakes like a queen! Also she sews better than her father and does a nice piece of embroidery too."

"Absolutely not!" cried Avram. "I know the girl! She's a shrew! Night and day she talks, nags, complains, cries, screams and carries on! Her father and mother can't wait to get rid of her. No thank you, not that one!"

"He could put cotton in his ears. For a cook like that!"

"Absolutely not!"

"What about Sonya? Such a pretty little thing. Her eyes are like stars, her lips are flowerbuds, her teeth — her teeth . . ."

The baker laughed. "You're crazy! She's a penniless orphan! A charity case!"

"What's wrong with an orphan? The boy won't have to worry about pleasing her family!"

"No, no, no," Avram said. "I had in mind a better match for this boy. Maybe Rivke, the rabbi's daughter?"

Velvel the Matchmaker put his hand to his head and rolled his eyes in disgust. "What are you talking about? She's worth a handsome young doctor or at the least a lawyer with a little money under the mattress. Please, her father would kick me out of the house if I brought in such a match! What about Sura?"

"She has a wart on her chin bigger than her nose!"

"A beauty mark. Just a beauty mark. Gittel?"

Avram threw his hands up. "Gittel? Gittel! Impossible! She's deaf and dumb!"

"I don't understand you, Avram!" cried Velvel. "Do you want a girl who talks? Take the tailor's youngest. You want a girl who *doesn't* talk? Take Gittel! Be reasonable — I'm offering everything under the sun!"

There was a long pause while the three men stared into their wine glasses. "Wait, wait — I have it! An absolute jewel, a beauty, a sweetheart!" The matchmaker was so excited he jumped up from his chair and danced around the room with his beard flying over his shoulder and his arms fanning the air. "You know who I'm thinking about? A wonderful girl! There isn't anything she can't do in the house. She makes wine, she makes cake, she sews, sweeps, scrubs! And a beauty? Prettier than Sonya. Eyes like the sun, they shine all the time! Such hair, such dainty hands and feet. A regular princess in disguise!"

Yankel's heart was pounding. His face broke out in a sweat and his hands shook with excitement. "Who? Who?" he cried. "Who?"

The matchmaker crooned in his delight, clapping his hands and swaying from side to side. Only Avram the Baker was perfectly calm. "You're talking about the Queen of Sheba maybe? Who?"

Velvel sat down and took another glass of wine to compose himself. The making of a match is an exhausting business. "Who?" he whispered. "You don't know? I have in mind for this darling boy no one else but Leah, the daughter of the widow Shena-Golde! What do you say to that, eh? Isn't that a prize?"

Well, if not exactly a prize — you can take it from me, who knows what a beauty is and what a beauty isn't, that this Leah was a little brown mouse of a girl — if not a prize, at least a possibility. You never met Shena-Golde, the widow with five daughters? A lovely woman, a big woman, and the girls — nice girls all of them, and good in the kitchen. So why weren't they all married off long ago? Because it's hard for a widow to get up a decent dowry for her daughters, and in such days who would marry a girl without a fat bag of gold? All right, if the girl was a raving beauty maybe she could bewitch a wealthy widower — but otherwise? No hope!

"So. That's something to think about," said Avram. "You think they'd take *him?*" And the baker and the matchmaker turned to look Yankel over from head to foot. The matchmaker shrugged. The baker scratched his head. "What can we lose by trying?" said Velvel. "If we don't ask too much — and besides, Leah is already twenty-six!"

"Twenty-six?" Yankel cried in dismay. "So old?"

The matchmaker clapped his hands. "What do you mean OLD? Twenty-six is young! She's just hatched, a little chicken hardly out of short skirts. And anyway, with an older woman you don't have so many troubles. She'll be grateful for a husband. She'll stay at home and stick to business. Wait a minute, I'll put on my boots, and we'll go right over. Shena-Golde said any time — come any time."

At the widow's house the news of their coming caused a hurricane. You know how news flies ahead of you! Before they set foot across the doorstep the kitchen had been swept, the table cleared, a fresh cloth spread, water set boiling for tea. The youngest daughter threw a shawl over her head and ran to a neighbor's house to borrow cakes. The second daughter gathered up her skirts and ran off to fetch her uncle so there should be a man in the house. Shena-Golde changed her apron; Leah changed her dress.

"Well, well!" cried the widow. "This is a surprise. Why didn't you let me know you were coming, Reb Velvel? The house is a mess! Well, you'll have to take us as we are!" And she cast a proud look around her spotless kitchen.

"Don't trouble yourself, aunty," the matchmaker said with a wave of his hand. And he whispered into the baker's ear, "Such a handsome woman. You can see what a housekeeper she is, ha?"

Then in came the uncle, panting and wiping his fat cheeks with a handkerchief, and everyone sat down to tea and talked about the weather.

You know how these things are. Arranging a match between a young man and a young woman is a very delicate thing. You don't just start out

56

making a bargain as though you were selling a cow and buying a horse. In fact, you talk about anything except the matter at hand. Of course, there are a few words thrown in — but wait, you'll see what I mean.

"Delicious cake," said Reb Velvel.

"A little dry, don't you think? My next door neighbor sent them over. Maybe I'm spoiled by Leah's baking. The way Leah bakes, if she made these she would throw them out in the yard for the chickens! Isn't that right, Leah?"

The girl, pouring tea, turned red. "Yes, Mama," she whispered.

"Listen to her!" cried the uncle. "Such an obedient, quiet little thing. A real old-fashioned girl. Listen, my dear — while I'm here would you mind sewing this button on my coat? You can see it's ready to fall off. My wife offered to do it, but I told her no, nobody can sew like my niece Leah!"

With great pity Yankel watched the poor girl trying to thread a needle in front of all those eyes. Her head was bent so low he could see nothing but the part in her dark hair. The thread went right and left, up and down — anywhere but through the eye of the needle. "I'll help you!" he cried, jumping out of his chair.

"He can do anything!" Velvel the Matchmaker crowed — just as if Yankel had walked on the ceiling. "He has golden hands!"

"A real marvel," the baker agreed. "You should see him working around the ovens — it's a pleasure to watch. And, of course," he added casually, "some day the business will be his."

The uncle perked up his ears. "Is that so? You don't have any sons, Reb Avram?"

"No sons and no daughters. My wife — God rest her soul, she died three years ago this past Monday — my wife and I prayed night and day for a family. But who am I to question the Lord's will?"

The widow Shena-Golde clucked in sympathy. "How is it you never got married again, Reb Avram? It's not right for a man to live alone."

"Who would marry an old man like me?" said the baker. "What could I offer a woman? It's true I have a good business and a nice little house with the yard full of geese and chickens — but who would have me? I don't fancy a young girl, to be perfectly frank with you. They're all so skinny these days." And here the baker looked with admiration at the widow's plump arms and her pink chins spilling one-two-three over the collar of her dress. "What's more," he went on, blushing like a schoolboy, "I'm afraid a young woman would run

me ragged. If I'm going to have a family I'll have to find one already made!"

And during all this talking, what was going on? Well, what do you think? Out of the corner of his eye Yankel was looking at Leah, and Leah was looking at Yankel, also sideways, as if it would break her neck if she moved her head.

The younger sisters, running back and forth with the kettle and the cakes — they, too, were looking hard enough to burn holes in Yankel's coat. Finally there was a little smile on this side, a little smile on that side, and as far as the young people were concerned, the match was as good as made.

Indeed it was. Within a day the news was all over the village. Avram the Baker and the widow Shena-Golde were to be wed before the month was out. "What about Leah?" cried Yankel to the baker.

The baker closed his eyes and rubbed his chin thoughtfully. "I have a little money set aside," he said, "and she's a good-looking girl. The match-maker tells me that Gimpel, the tailor's sister's son is looking for a wife. He's a smart boy, that Gimpel — he could be a help around the bakery — and who knows, maybe he'll take over, and Shena-Golde and I could go sit in the sun."

"And what about me?" cried Yankel, biting his lip.

"Be reasonable!" said Avram the Baker.

What misery! Do you want to hear any more? Poor Yankel went to plenty of weddings that year — and none of them were his.

Well, whatever people say, there must be a cup or two of justice in this world — and not only in the next. Just let me tell you that Gimpel, Avram's new son-in-law, was a first-class ox around the ovens. He ruined half the dough, and he nearly ruined the baker into the bargain. But what's the good of such justice? Who does it help?

VI. YANKEL THE THIEF

Start a cart rolling downhill and soon even the horse can't stop it! That's how things were with Yankel — rolling from bad to worse — and always faster.

He had set his heart on marrying Leah, poor Schlimazel. There were times when — if it hadn't been for his old grandmother — Yankel might have thrown himself into the river. Such despair! He didn't know what to do with himself. He didn't care. He lost his appetite and grew skinnier than ever. In the morning he couldn't find the strength to rise. At bedtime he couldn't find the peace to sleep. Soon he fell into the habit of roaming the village at night, looking for sleep as a lost soul searches for its body.

It's no joke to wander around in the dark of the moon. A good citizen hurrying home late from his work walks quickly and murmurs his prayers. How do you know whom you'll meet? There are stories! They say the dead sometimes visit the places they knew in their lifetimes — and they say much worse! But why should I frighten you with such tales? Forget I ever mentioned them. You'll rest easier. Just let me assure you that when Yankel roamed the streets he went without human company!

One icy night, when the village was closed up like a jack-in-the-box, Yankel slipped out of the house and made his way toward the river to sit there on the bank until sleep came to greet him. He walked with his hands tucked into his armpits, his shoulders hunched against the cold, his head down. The human world was deadly quiet. A restless wind moaned up and down the empty streets, rattling the shutters and trying the doors — aching to get inside.

Suddenly, turning a corner, he bumped headlong into a dark shape, knocking it to the ground.

If his feet had not frozen numb on the spot, Yankel would have been home and under the covers before he drew another breath.

"God help me!" cried a human voice. "What do you want?"

So it was a man? Was that all?

"What do I want?" muttered Yankel, more to himself than to anyone else. "What is there I don't want? I am in want of everything!"

"God save me!" the fallen man cried again. "Don't kill me, I beg you. I'm a father ten times over, and who will feed my family if I am dead? Let me go and you can have everything! Here — here is my purse!" And pressing his treasures into Yankel's hands, the poor father of ten scrambled to his feet and ran down the street as if all the demons of hell were chasing him.

"Wait!" Yankel called. "Wait!" There was no answer but the sound of feet running faster.

The moneybag weighed heavy in Yankel's hand, and he peeked inside, counting by the light of the pale moon — five, ten, fifteen copper coins — and look at that — two gold rubles!

"Well, that's a good haul!" said Yankel to himself. "If it's that easy to be a thief, a thief I will be. It hurts less than starving — and I'm already used to the hours!" Then he made his way home to bed at once, before some real thief came out of the shadows to relieve him of his prize!

You hear this, my friend angel? You understand that as far as Yankel's part in it went, it was all a mistake. So who is at fault?

There are two possibilities. Either it was God's hand pushing that purse into Yankel's fingers — or it was the devil's.

If it was God's hand — and why would he do a thing like that? I can't believe it, it's impossible!

Then again, if it was the devil's hand, there are two further possibilities. Either the devil wished to test Yankel — or he wished to test you.

If the devil had Yankel in mind, it's very clear that the poor unhappy boy was in no position to resist the temptation. Why didn't you help him? Surely you're responsible!

If, on the other hand, the devil had you in mind, my fine feathered friend — !

So who is at fault? Believe me, I have more than half a mind to report you!

Now, every night when his grandmother was asleep, Yankel set out for work. He wrapped himself in a big ragged black cloak and rubbed his face and hands with soot from the chimney.

Quietly, quietly he went through the village, staying close to the shadows, searching for an open door or a shutter left ajar. If the house was unlocked he was soon inside it, taking what he could to stuff into his sack.

One night, in the hours just before dawn, Yankel slipped through a half-open window into the house of a rich woman — the widow of a grain merchant. He found many things to his liking — a fat loaf of white bread, a bag of apples, a copper pitcher and a silver plate.

But where were the widow's jewels? Where was the necklace she wore on holidays? The big gold earrings he had seen dangling from her ears? He lit a candle and searched every cupboard and chest — and still he found none of them.

He was in such a hurry to get through with his work before the cocks began to crow that he made more and more noise in his search — until finally he woke the old lady. She was about to set up a racket — scream for help — but Yankel kept his head. "Quiet!" he commanded. "I've taken hardly anything. If I'd known what rubbish you had here I wouldn't have bothered to come out tonight!"

The widow was so insulted that she lost her fear immediately! "Rubbish?" she cried. "My husband, God rest his soul, never gave me anything but the finest!" Yankel laughed. "Look!" cried the widow and she reached under her pillow and brought out her holiday necklace. "Pure gold! The best! Look at that chain! So fine the angels couldn't make better!" Yankel smiled and waved his hand as if this were nothing. "The rabbi's wife has better!"

"What?" said the widow, jumping out of bed. "Does the rabbi's wife have anything to match *this*?" And she pried loose a stone from the fireplace and brought out from its secret place a locked wooden box. "Look at these earrings! Look at this bracelet! Here is a ring that the Queen of Sheba would have envied. THIS you call rubbish? My husband, God rest his soul, would turn in his grave to hear you talk!"

Very intently Yankel studied the treasures the widow heaped in his hands, dangling them one by one in front of the candle flame. "Ummmmmm," he said. "Uh-huh!" he said. Then, leaning close to the candle, he pursed his lips and cried, "W-w-w-w-well!" and the flame was out and Yankel out after it.

"Robber!" shrieked the widow. "Thief! Help me! Save me!"

Yankel hid behind a water barrel as the neighbors came running from their houses to help the old woman. They searched the street, looked up

the chimney, peered under the bed. Why couldn't they find him? Because he was in the neighbors' houses while they were in the street — stuffing his sack and laughing until he couldn't see for the tears in his eyes!

In order to sell his stolen goods Yankel went once a week to a certain inn, many miles outside of the village, a hangout for thieves, cutthroats and highwaymen.

To this place the trader came. This trader was a deaf, bent, wispy-bearded man with a sackful of gold and a pocketful of copper coins. The old man was particularly fond of Yankel, and you can guess why without a second guess. From Yankel he made a tidy profit — never giving him more than a few kopeks for jewels worth many rubles and often talking him out of the best of his bag.

As much as the trader loved Yankel, that's how much Yankel hated the trader. He knew he was being cheated right and left. One day he decided to do something really crazy. He made up his mind to lie in wait for the trader just at the edge of the woods and jump on him when he passed, take his sackful of stolen goods and his money and leave him with empty hands. So he bought a gun.

The woods were dark and damp. Yankel

wrapped himself in his cloak and tucked the gun into his belt. Then he climbed a tree and settled himself in the crotch of two branches with his legs dangling. By the time he saw the trader making his way along the stony path, Yankel was sore and stiff, touched with mildew and in a vile temper.

"Stop!" Yankel roared, jumping out of the tree and waving his gun.

"What?" said the old man.

"Give me your money," Yankel shouted.

"What?" said the old man. "What?"

"Give me your money or I'll shoot you!"

The old man shrugged. "Don't make fun of me, Yankel. You know I'm deaf!"

Yankel stuck the gun in the trader's face. "You may be deaf," he screamed at the top of his lungs, "but you have two eyes! See the gun? The gun! I'll shoot you with the gun if you don't give me your bag!"

The man's face lit up. "Aaaah!" he said. "You want to sell me the gun, Yankel? Why didn't you say so? If it works I'll give you a good price."

Yankel was thoroughly vexed. "NO!" he howled.

"Oh-ho!" the old man said. "So it doesn't work? Trying to cheat your old friend? That's not nice!"

One, two, three — Yankel fired into the air. "HEAR THAT?"

"You'll have to come a little closer," said the trader calmly, as if nothing were going on. "And talk a little louder, if you please."

Yankel grabbed the man by the front of his jacket and let off another volley of shots. "I SAID IT WORKS!" he shouted.

"What? What?" said the man. "I didn't hear a thing!"

"Listen, you old fool!" Yankel screamed into the trader's ear. He pulled the trigger again — and nothing happened. There wasn't a bullet left.

Quick as a ferret the trader turned his head and clamped his teeth on Yankel's nose. The young man let out a scream, and the empty gun flew out of his hand. From behind him an arm clamped around his neck, and a rock came down on his head. The cutthroats at the inn, hearing screams and shots, had come running to see what was going on. They knew who buttered their bread, and they were all on the trader's side. In a few minutes Yankel was beaten up so badly that blood poured from him like wine from a broken cask.

The old trader paid his friends handsomely for their help and started on his way again. "You dirty goat!" muttered Yankel through his broken teeth. Far down the path the old man turned. "Watch your tongue, Yankel, my boy!" he said pleasantly.

"Have some respect for the old!" And he strolled off, humming to himself like a man without an enemy in this world.

VII. YANKEL AND THE
WONDER-WORKING RABBI

What a story! Isn't that enough to tear your heart
out? Here's a man who's worked all his life like a
dog — and what happens? He gets treated like a
dog! Is that fair? The whole world is against him!

I could make things turn out better than that, if
you want to know my opinion. Yes, if you want to
know my opinion, I've already worked out a very
nice ending to the story.

Listen, my angel friend — I'll tell you what I have in mind and you judge. If it suits you, speak to somebody. I don't need much to work with. Give me one white goat and a wonder-working rabbi, and I'll have it fixed up in no time!

The village is in an uproar because the Wonder-working Rabbi is coming. With his followers he travels from town to town, and everywhere he goes there is great celebration — dancing and singing and eating. He brings joy with him, along with his luggage. Everybody has heard about his wisdom, his humility, his ability to perform miracles. When Rabbi Menachem is in your village it's another place entirely, I tell you. Everything is cleaner and brighter. The people are friendlier. Even the little babies forget about yelling and let their mothers sleep through the night!

As soon as the news comes everybody sets out to get ready. The holiday clothing is spread out in the fresh air, the houses are white-washed inside and out, fresh earth is brought in and beaten down to make the floors clean and smooth and even the streets are swept. The baker's ovens never grow cold, the tailor sews by candlelight until dawn, the shoemaker eats at his bench. It's hard to believe — but the beggars wash their feet and their faces.

Yankel's grandmother is beside herself with excitement. Her crippled fingers can hardly hold a needle, but she sits in the sun and patches their best clothes. Her grandson is driving her crazy. He sleeps all day, and she has to nag him to do a little around the house. What's the matter with the boy? He has no interest in anything. If you told him the Messiah was coming he would stretch his arms and yawn!

Finally he fixes the shutters. He puts a few nails in the door. The grandmother tears apart an old dress to make curtains. She counts her kopeks. So much for a fish. So much for noodles. Maybe she can squeeze out enough for a fresh egg?

Finally the day arrives. A man on horseback gallops into the village with sweat pouring over his face. It's the tailor. He's so excited his tongue trips over his teeth. The rabbi's wife rushes out of her house with a glass of wine to calm him. What's the news? What's happening? He was on the way to town with a new suit for the doctor's brother's son, who's finally getting married after all these years, and halfway there he met the Wonder-working Rabbi and his followers. Right away he turned around and hurried back. Let the doctor's nephew get married next week. He waited this long, he can wait a little longer. Now the tailor rushes off

to his house. Is everything ready? They'll be here by sundown!

After supper the youngest children are sent to the edge of town as lookouts. They see the carriage come and they run through the streets shouting. Their high little voices are like pipes. He's here! Toot-a-loot! He's here!

Everybody gapes. Look at that carriage! It's polished so brightly it could be silver-plated. And the rabbi himself — can you believe it? His coat is velvet, embroidered all over with flowers and trimmed with fur — top and bottom, tied with a silk cord.

There's so much fur on his hat that you can't see if it's velvet or satin. And in the middle of this finery the great Rabbi Menachem is like a raisin in a bun — dark, wrinkled, no bigger than a child. His eyes turn right and left. They are searchlights, lightning bolts, glowing coals in his face. He looks at you, and you step back and press your hand to your chest.

Tiny fingers dart out from the wide cuffs and part his curly white beard, and there is a cherry of a mouth. His tongue flicks out and moistens his lips. He looks around. He looks around. Who's breathing? Rabbi Menachem smiles! He laughs! Out loud! And all in an instant everyone in the crowd is laughing and crying, pressing forward, clapping their hands, leaning to touch the Wonder-working Rabbi. He is offered a dozen houses to sleep in, more dinners than the tsar's army could eat in a month. But it's all arranged. A house has been made ready for them. With dainty steps, a clucking attendant at each elbow, the great rabbi leads the way. The crowd follows. Only Yankel, leaning against the wall of the stable, stays behind.

What's in Yankel's mind? Business, of course. Don't tell me bad times make good fellows. Here's Yankel who was a boy with a golden heart and what is he now? He's a thief. First and last a thief. There's no pleasure in that. Already he's planning on how he can get into the house at night, how big a sack he'll need, who'll buy a velvet coat embroidered all over with flowers.

The hours in-between are nothing to us. It's after midnight now, and everybody has gone to bed, exhausted. The Wonder-working Rabbi is floating on goose-down pillows while his followers lie on rough benches in the next room. They too could be sleeping in comfort but they want to be near, to stay near, their master.

Slowly the shutter swings open. Yankel has taken care to see to it that the lock on that window won't close properly. It's hard to squeeze through the tiny hole, but Yankel gets in without a sound.

He's afraid to light a candle. He spreads his sack on the floor and squints so his eyes will become used to the dark. The rabbi breathes softly, like an infant. In the next room the men snore and turn. Their noises will cover the sound of the creeping thief. Ah, if there were only a moon — a little glow of light.

A gentle cough. Yankel's eyes dart toward the bed. There is the rabbi, sitting bolt upright with his beard spilling over the coverlet, his hands folded neatly on his lap. "What is it, my boy?" he whispers. Why is he whispering? He should shout. He should scream. His followers would be in before Yankel could get out the window. "Have you come to steal?" whispers the old man. "Aside from my clothing you won't find much. You want my fur hat?" He seems amused.

Yankel's voice is harsh. It scrapes out of his throat. "Money!" he says. The rabbi laughs softly. "I give it to the poor." He swings his legs over the side of the bed and stands on the floor in his nightgown, his feet bare. Yankel's hands twist together — the old rabbi is no bigger than his grandmother, and he's frail. Little arms, little legs. Like a chicken without feathers.

"Sit down!" says the rabbi. There is a table, a

carved wooden table, two chairs. There is a bottle of wine on the table. The rabbi uncorks the wine and pours two glasses. One he hands to Yankel. Yankel sits down. He doesn't know what else to do. He's afraid to run and unwilling to hurt the old man. He's at the rabbi's mercy.

The rabbi leans close to Yankel, and his breath is sweet with the smell of the wine. "Why are you doing this?" he asks. "Why do you want to be a thief?"

There are tears in Yankel's eyes. "Who wants to be a thief?" he cries. "I'm a thief because I can't be anything else. I can't make a living being the village fool!"

"Ah!" says the old man. "And what makes you think you're a fool?"

"What makes me think that? It's drummed into my ears night and day. Everybody knows it, and they don't wait to tell me!"

"And you believe them? What a fool you are!"

"If only I had your brains!"

"What God didn't give you, I can't give you. What else?"

So Yankel gives over his troubles one by one, with plenty of tears. "And finally," he cries, "I would have to be named Schlimazel! Bad luck follows me around like a billy goat, butting may back-

side — morning, noon and night! How can I run away from that?" And he bursts into sobs against the rabbi's shoulder.

"Shah, shah!" the old man murmurs, stroking Yankel's hand. So they sit like this for half an hour. It is plain that the rabbi is thinking. At last he reaches some satisfactory conclusion. "Look, my boy," he says gently. "Go home and get some sleep. Morning is wiser than evening. Tomorrow is time enough for working wonders!"

Yankel jumps up. "You have a miracle for me?" he cries out. "For me?"

"Sometimes," the old rabbi says with a smile, "men are more than they seem and miracles are less. Tomorrow, God willing, you will be a wise man with a lucky name. But tomorrow — not to-night. Now I will tell you what to do. Listen carefully, eh?"

VIII. MAZEL TOV

So! Now it's morning, and the rabbi is eating his breakfast. Already there is a crowd outside the door — and inside, it's bedlam. Everybody of importance is there. Our village rabbi, the doctor, Velvel the Matchmaker, the millionaire from America — everybody. And all in their holiday clothes. The rabbi says nothing. He chews his food. He sips his tea. All of a sudden he jumps up and looks around the room.

"Where's Mazel tov?" he cries. What's this?

What is he saying? Mazel tov? Mazel tov means "good luck." That's what you say when a baby is born, when there's a wedding, when your friend gets an inheritance. It's nobody's name.

The rabbi is still standing up looking around. "Where's Mazel tov?" One of the rabbi's followers runs to the door. "Is there anybody here named Mazel tov?" he asks. Not now, not ever in the history of the village was there anybody named Mazel tov outside that house. The rabbi is very disturbed. "I had a dream last night," he says, and everybody is silent.

"I was fast asleep, and suddenly something woke me. There was a huge black billy goat standing by the side of my bed. I tell you my heart jumped into my mouth. I started saying my prayers as fast as I could. Who else could it be but the devil himself? I have to go over my sins. What particular sin does he want me for?

"Finally I come to a pause in the prayers. 'Who are you?' I cry, 'What do you want with me?'

"The goat has a runny nose. He snuffles when he talks. 'My name is Schlimazel, and I'm looking for my master.'

"Look, I'm a stranger in town, and how should I know who his master is? But I think fast. 'Why are you looking for him here?' I say. 'I saw him

86

leaving the village with a pack on his back, on his way to see the tsar. Hurry up and catch up with him — and if you get there first, hang around until he comes.' As far as I'm concerned the tsar can have this goat, Schlimazel, forever!"

Outside the house people are climbing on each other's shoulders, trying to see the Wonder-working Rabbi. Every word out of his mouth is handed from one to the next until the little children on the edge get the story. The rabbi continues.

"So I'm just drifting off to sleep again when I hear a sound outside my window. I open the shutters and peer out into the street. There's a white nanny goat standing there — a pretty little thing with flowers wound around her neck and she greets me nicely. 'Excuse me, Rabbi Menachem, for disturbing your rest. I'm Mazel tov. My master just died. He was a hundred and seventy-nine years old, and he went straight to heaven. Before he left he called me to his side. "Go to such and such a village," he said, "and find your new master. If you get stuck, look for Rabbi Menachem and ask his advice." So here I am, and what can you tell me?'

"What could I tell her? 'Wait,' I say, 'until the sun comes up. Morning is wiser than evening.'

"For this piece of advice, if you can call it advice, the little goat thanks me politely, and in turn she advises me to get into bed again before I catch a chill, which I do — and that is the last I think of it until this very moment! So where is Mazel tov? Who has seen the goat of my dreams?"

Nobody. Of course nobody. But straightaway a dozen men push their way out of the room and start searching the town. "Mazel tov!" they shout. "Mazel tov!"

And who is this coming along the road? It's Yankel, our poor Schlimazel! He's been following the rabbi's instructions to the letter. Before dawn he was out of bed and trotting off to the farm of a peasant a few miles from town. And as the rabbi told him to do he bought a little white nanny goat, and as the rabbi told him, he has twined her neck with wild flowers.

What a darling goat, what a beauty! What a prize to have for his very own! It's a wonder they got back into town, the two of them. Every few minutes Yankel has to stop and pet the little goat, to arrange the flowers. Now he hears the men calling. He looks up. They're running toward him, shouting. What's this they're saying? Mazel tov! Mazel tov! Something wonderful must have happened while he was gone. "Mazel tov!" he calls back. It's only polite! He pulls the ear of the little

white goat lovingly. "It's a sign." He says, "I'll call you Mazel tov — good luck!"

The men are all around him, tugging on his sleeve, talking all together, like a gaggle of geese when the housewife comes out with an apron full of feed. What's the name of this goat? What do you call her? Why, Mazel tov — isn't she a darling? And he can neither say yes nor no, but he's pushed and shoved, half carried into the room where the rabbi is having breakfast. The rabbi claps his hands. He kisses Yankel on both cheeks. He makes a big to-do over the goat, as if it were a dear relative. Yankel is settled on the bench next to the rabbi — a plate is set for him — a glass of tea is put in his hand. He opens his mouth to say something — and he gets from the rabbi, under the table, such a pinch on the behind that his mouth snaps shut.

"Good morning, Reb Mazel tov," says the rabbi sweetly.

You would suppose somebody in that room would burst out laughing! You would suppose somebody would cry, "That's Yankel the Fool!" Don't think Yankel isn't waiting for such a thing. But the Wonder-working Rabbi has them all bewitched. The men are crushing each other to death in order to get a closer look at this Yankel who was chosen above all others by good fortune and a white nanny goat. And outside the door a space is hurriedly made for the old grandmother so she can see too.

Rabbi Menachem pushes away his plate and brushes the crumbs off the table. One of his followers places a leather-bound book on the cloth in front of him. The book is so huge that the old man couldn't possibly lift it himself.

In silence the old man studies the writing, nodding to himself now and then. Now he comes to a passage that seems to confound him, and he goes over it and over it, his lips moving and his finger following each word on the page. The crowd doesn't bother him. They are scarcely breathing, scarcely moving. What it is he studies they have no idea, but it is a great privilege just to be in the room with all his wisdom.

Suddenly he turns to Yankel who sits as still as a turtle on the bench beside him. "I have a problem," says Rabbi Menachem in a high, clear voice. "This book is in an ancient language and not always clear to me. Here it reads 'And the angel asked the king where his father dwelled.' Then there is the king's answer, which I cannot make out, and the angel speaks again. 'Because he was given over into your care.' Please, Reb Mazel tov, will you be kind enough to translate this line for me?"

Poor Yankel. His eyes pop out of his head in terror. What kind of a trick is this rabbi about to play on him? Who is he, the village fool, who can neither read nor write, to translate ancient languages for the learned rabbi? He breaks out into a sweat. "Why do you ask *me*?" he cries.

The rabbi laughs in delight. "Yes, yes!" he cries, "How foolish of me. That's exactly it!"

"And the angel asked the king where his father dwelled. And the king says, 'Why do you ask *me*?' The angel replies, 'Because he was given over into your care!' "

Ah, so perfectly simple! The millionaire from America looks at the doctor, the doctor looks at the baker. Who would have guessed? Such wisdom in one so young! "Very good, Reb Mazel tov!" somebody calls out.

The village is delighted to have discovered a scholar in its midst. The old grandmother is covered with kisses. A space is found for her inside the house. She gets a stool to sit on. But breakfast is over. Rabbi Menachem will retire to study.

A man presses forward and asks a word with the rabbi. It seems he has had an argument with a neighbor about some wheat. Will the good Rabbi Menachem, the wise rabbi, be kind enough to hear all the facts and decide the merits of the case? Of course, of course — a little later. This afternoon. There are other people who have such problems. Later, later. Come back later. This afternoon everything will be taken care of. Rabbi Menachem and Reb Mazel tov will settle everything.

The rabbi goes into the bedroom and because he has clamped his hand around Yankel's wrist, Yankel follows.

As soon as the door is closed, Yankel falls to his knees and kisses the hem of Rabbi Menachem's velvet coat. "You are a saint!" he cries. "A miracle worker!"

"I am a trickster and a rogue!" says the rabbi. He doesn't seem particularly sorry.

They sit down at the table. Yankel creases his brow. "Rabbi," he says, "what am I going to do when the elders come to me and ask me to settle an argument? One says the book says this, one says the book says that. How am I to know if I can neither read nor write?"

"It's simple," says the rabbi. "You turn to a third man and ask, 'What do you think?' And, of course, he tells you. And you agree. You say, 'Indeed, that is my thought also.' In that way two men are made to feel wise and only one is wrong!"

"Rabbi Menachem," Yankel cries. "How am I going to help settle the dispute over the wheat?"

"It's simple," says the rabbi. "Remember a few easy rules: No one may keep what is not rightfully his.

"When there is doubt, divide everything evenly.

"A bargain is a bargain.

"You understand? It's simple. These rules will cover everything. And if they do not, why, then you turn to a third man and ask his opinion, eh?"

The rabbi and the young man sit side by side on the bench. The first case to be settled is the one regarding the wheat. This man Beryl bought a basket of wheat from his neighbor Shimon. Half of the basket is indeed good wheat. At the bottom there are pebbles. It's a fraud!

Rabbi Menachem whispers in Yankel's ear. The first rule.

Yankel clears his throat. "You," he says to Beryl, "bought wheat. You did not agree to buy stones, and you did not pay for stones. No one may keep what is not his. Therefore, you" — and he points to Shimon — "will stand against the wall of the house and your friend Beryl will throw your stones back to you, one by one."

The dishonest neighbor turns pale, and his hands twist together. He has no wish to be stoned. "I will give Beryl a full measure of wheat. He may keep the stones as a present from me!" And he runs out of the house in a panic. Everybody laughs.

"You're a wise man, Reb Mazel tov!" says Beryl. "Please be kind enough to accept this coin for your trouble."

The next case. Two brothers. The younger one falls to his knees. "My father, on his deathbed, left the house to me."

The older brother stands with his arms folded. He throws his head back and looks down his nose. "That's not right. The house is mine too. How could he disinherit *me*, his eldest son?"

Rabbi Menachem nudges Yankel. The second rule. Yankel leans his elbows on the table and touches the tips of his fingers together. He nods. He creases his brow. "You are right," he says to the older man. "Everything must be evenly divided. Half the house is yours. The walls belong to your younger brother, but you may have the roof!"

"What?" the man cries. "What good is a roof without walls under it? I don't want the roof!"

"Very good," Yankel says. "Then the entire house is your brother's."

"You're a wise man, Reb Mazel tov. Here's a ruble for your troubles," says the younger brother.

Now what is it?

"When I married my Roisl, her father promised me a hundred rubles to set myself up in business. Now he won't pay. It's been seven years. I have five children to support."

"A bargain is a bargain," says Yankel. The third rule. "Give back your wife. And the children, of course."

The young man looks stunned. The girl's father stamps his feet. "I don't want her back! What will I do with a divorced woman and five children?"

"How should I know?" says Yankel with a shrug. "Buy her a new husband."

"It would cost me a fortune," the man complains. "It's cheaper to pay my son-in-law the hundred rubles."

"Reb Mazel tov, you're a man of wisdom. I'll give you a fat goose and a basket of eggs!" says the husband. "I'll bake you a cake!" cries the young wife.

And who is last? Our own rabbi has a complaint against Reb Velvel the Matchmaker. Rivke, the rabbi's daughter, is of an age to marry. In fact she's been of an age to marry for some time. She's getting a little old, to tell the truth. The matchmaker has promised to find her a husband, a man of standing in the community, a man of some worth. A scholar. For his expenses our village rabbi has advanced Reb Velvel considerable money.

So. A few years back it seemed as if everything were arranged. An engagement was announced between Rivke and the doctor's nephew. Then some facts came to light. I won't even repeat them — a regular scandal. Of course, the engagement was broken.

Now Reb Velvel brings forward only old men, foolish men, men of no consequence. He won't give back the money our rabbi has laid out — and what's worse, he can't seem to find the girl a husband. It's a knotty problem.

Yankel searches for a rule that will cover this case. He turns to Rabbi Menachem, the Wonder-working Rabbi. "What do you think? What's your opinion?"

Rabbi Menachem purses his little cherry lips and looks into the air. "It seems to me that *you* should marry the girl."

"My opinion exactly," cries Yankel. Then he grabs the edge of the table to keep from falling off the bench. What's this? What's been said?

He looks at this girl, Rivke, the rabbi's daughter. She's a beauty! Her long braids sit like blackbirds on her shoulders. Her cheeks are flushed and her eyes are lowered modestly.

"Of course," says the Wonder-working Rabbi, "if I were you, I would hold out for a good dowry. All the household furnishings. Enough cash money to buy the bakery from Reb Avram. No less than four pillows of the best white goose down." He looks up from under his eyebrows at the girl's father. This crafty old man has our village rabbi in a daze. "Of course, of course," murmurs our rabbi, and Rivke lifts her head and gives Yankel such a smile that his blood dances.

"Mazel tov!" cries the doctor. "Mazel tov!" the crowd shouts back. What kissing and crying and carrying on! The wedding will be at once. Rabbi Menachem will marry the young couple. There will be a feast such as there never was in this world or the other! Somebody steps back against Yankel's pretty white goat. "Naaaaaaaah!" she bleats. And the millionaire from America picks her up and sets her on the table.

Rabbi Menachem grabs Yankel, Yankel grabs his grandmother, the grandmother grabs Rivke, Rivke grabs her father. Round and round they go, dancing their joy — round and round the table, while the little goat Mazel tov throws back her head and sings the tune.

So why not, my friend angel? How much trouble would it be for you up there in heaven, who can do anything you please, to provide me with one white nanny goat and one Wonder-working Rabbi? You have a certain responsibility for this boy, don't you? Don't shake your head, my friend — we've already discussed all this. It's very clear!

And think what a party it will mean in heaven!

After all, it will be *your* doing, and you'll get to sit at the head of the table, to choose the best piece of chicken, to drink the first glass of wine.

The best piece of chicken! So. So? What do you say?

Author-illustrator SHAN ELLENTUCK was born in Brooklyn and, as she puts it, grew up in the Brooklyn Museum and in the main branch of the Brooklyn Public Library. This atmosphere gave her a rich background in literature and art.

Mrs. Ellentuck received her art training at the Brooklyn Museum school, the New York Art Students League, and Pratt Institute. She has been a designer of stained glass and museum displays and has both written and illustrated several books for children, including *The Upside-Down Man, Did You See What I Said?* and *A Sunflower as Big as the Sun,* which was an Honor Book in the 1968 Children's Spring Book Festival. During the past two years she has worked in the Brooklyn school system in a program to encourage creative writing.

Mrs. Ellentuck and her architect husband, Bert, live in Roosevelt, New Jersey, with their four children, three cats, a dog and a white rabbit.